Focus

The focus of this book is:

- to read information from maps,
- to answer questions using text and illustra...

Tuning In

The front cover

Read the title.

What do you expect this book to be about?

The back cover

Read the blurb on the back cover. This book has maps which will give us information about where Joe is.

Contents

What is this page called?

What information does it give us?

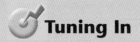 **Tuning In**

Which city did Joe visit?

Who do you think took the photographs?

Joe's Trip

Joe went to London for the day. He visited lots of places.

 Prompt and Praise

Check that the children have read all the captions and looked at the symbols for the famous places.

Speaking and Listening

Have you visited any of these places?

These are the places Joe saw.
He took photographs of them all.

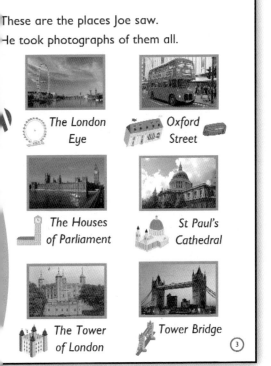

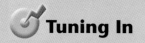
Tuning In

Where did Joe go first? What is Joe saying?

The London Eye

First Joe went to the London Eye.
Find it on the map.

I saw all of London from the London Eye.

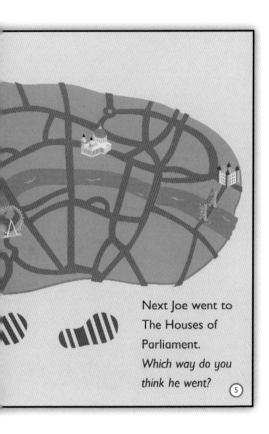

Next Joe went to The Houses of Parliament. Which way do you think he went?

 Prompt and Praise

Check that the children can locate places on the map and follow the route.

Speaking and Listening

Why could he see all of London? Look on the map and find where he went next. Which route did he take?

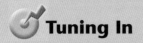

Tuning In

Find The Houses of Parliament on the map. How did Joe get from the London Eye to The Houses of Parliament?

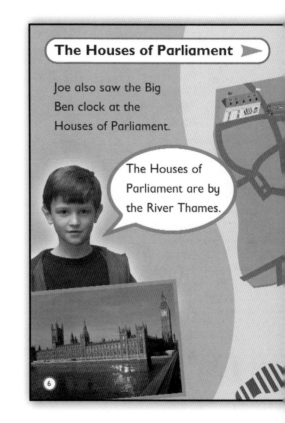

The Houses of Parliament

Joe also saw the Big Ben clock at the Houses of Parliament.

The Houses of Parliament are by the River Thames.

 Prompt and Praise

Check that the children have read all the information on the pages.

Speaking and Listening

Where did Joe go next? Look back at page 3 to find out. What is Joe's next picture after The Houses of Parliament? Which way did he go?

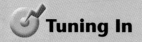
Tuning In

Where is Oxford Street?

How did Joe get from The Houses of Parliament to Oxford Street?

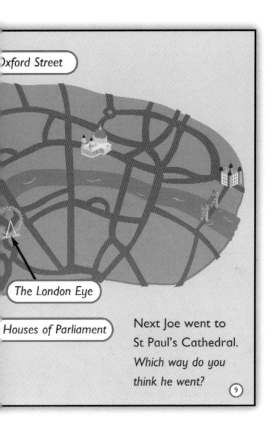

Next Joe went to St Paul's Cathedral. Which way do you think he went?

 Prompt and Praise

Check that the children can read all the proper nouns.

Speaking and Listening

Where did Joe go next? Which way did he go?

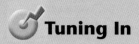
Tuning In

Find St Paul's Cathedral, which way did he go from Oxford Street to St Paul's Cathedral?

St Paul's Cathedral

Joe climbed the steps to the very top of St Paul's Cathedral.

St Paul's Cathedral has a huge dome.

Next Joe went to the Tower of London. Which way do you think he went?

 Prompt and Praise

Check that the children have read the speech bubble.

Speaking and Listening

What is special about St Paul's Cathedral?

Look at page 3 to find out where Joe went next.

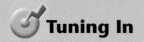 **Tuning In**

Look at the photo Joe is holding. What did Joe notice about The Tower of London?

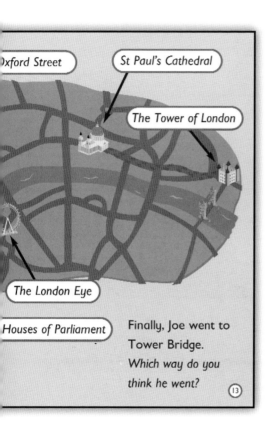

Finally, Joe went to Tower Bridge. Which way do you think he went?

 Prompt and Praise

Check that the children locate each place on the map.

Speaking and Listening

Find the London Eye and trace Joe's journey to The Tower of London.

What is the last place Joe went to?

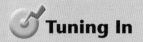
Tuning In

Find Tower Bridge on the map.

How did Joe get from The Tower of London to Tower Bridge?

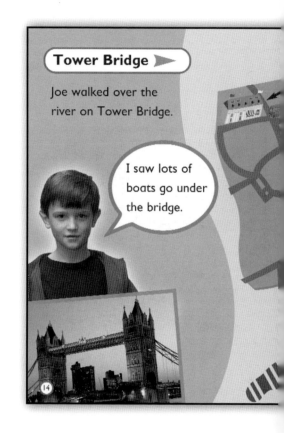

 Prompt and Praise

Check that the children locate each place on the map.

Speaking and Listening

What is the picture on page 15 telling us? What was the first place Joe visited? Trace his journey to the next places he went.

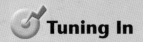 **Tuning In**

What is this map showing us?

Joe lives in Leeds. Find it on the map.

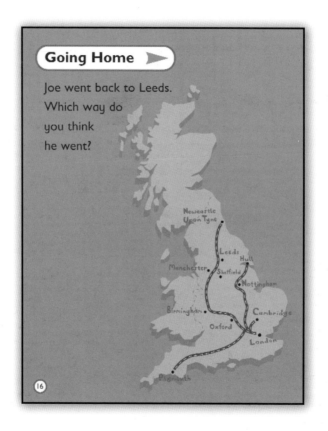

 Prompt and Praise

Check that the children understand where they live on the map.

Speaking and Listening

How did Joe get from London to Leeds?

Do we live closer to London than Joe or further away?